# DEADBEATS

# THANK YOU TO THE ECLECTIC PROJECTS PATRONS!

**This chapbook is produced and supported by the patrons of the Eclectic Projects Fund.**

Peter would like to extend his thanks to Margaret Ball, Kate Eltham, Jodi, Nicole Strickland, Meg Vann, Sally, Jennifer White, Maggie Slater, Tansy Rayner Roberts, Dave Versace; Catherine Caine, Kathleen Jennings, Stephanie Gunn, and Lois Spangler for their encouragement and support.

# DEADBEATS

## A HELIX CITY SHORT STORY

### PETER M. BALL

Eclectic Projects (an imprint of Brain Jar Press)
PO Box 6687
Upper Mt Gravatt, QLD, 4122
Australia
Eclectic Projects: www.PeterMBall.com
Brain Jar Press: www.BrainJarPress.com



Cover design by Brain Jar Press
Cover Images: Cryochamber with human body © Roman3dArt/Shutterstock.

ISBN: 978-1-922479-23-5 (Ebook) | 978-1-922479-24-2 (Chapbook)

# DEADBEATS

Cody's seated in Tennyson's Grindhouse when the first message comes through: briefing, 5:00. Fucking Bellamy throwing his his weight around, confident that he owns her. Cody Jones glares at it a couple of seconds, puts the phone away. Figures, what the hell, and orders another drink. One final glass of the cheap rocket-fuel that masquerades as booze, brewed in canisters in the basement of the Grindhouse. Tastes like shit, but it's potent, and potent matters more that flavour in this stretch of Downside, pressed up against the grimy shore of the river, all the squats and gangs and homeless communes living on the scraps Cityside throws out.

Cody Jones nurses the drink and contemplates her debts. Thinks about the job and the hangover waiting for her when she's on the right side of sober, and the fact she still can't sleep right even all these years after her decanting.

She drinks.

It doesn't help.

So she orders another.

．　．　．

Cody figures it for 12:40, given the crowd packed onto the Boundary Road. She's tired and hungover and heading home, trying to blend in with the crush of bodies: worn jeans and a black t-shirt, sunglasses over bloodshot eyes, her stomach still burning through the last of Tennyson's liquor. A foul breeze rifles through the stunted buildings, brings with it the petrochemical stink of the river. Cody slinks down the Boundary, takes a left at the wreckage of the first Valhalla Bar. Weaves through the street-markets, dodging elbows and shouting vendors, Cityside Tourists looking for bargains and taking in the local colour. There's a rat-boy working a grill at the base of her squat, young kid still on his first run of gene-morphs, stubby tail hanging through a hole in his jeans and fuzzy grey down covering his cheeks. The aroma of the mystery meat roils against her stomach, reminds her how long it's been since she ate.

She crouches, points. "What?"

The rat-boy shrugs, holds up two fingers, doesn't bother identifying the source of his protein. Cody weighs up the odds, hands over her money. Walks away with two bamboo skewers in hand, the grey meat pasted with a chilli-flecked sauce that glistens in the afternoon light. She wolfs the first stick down, lets the gamey meat wage war with the sick feeling in her guts. When it stays down, she takes her time with the second, rips free small mouthfuls as she climbs the stairs.

Sweat clings to her forehead by the time she hits the top floor and thumbs her code into the keypad with a grease-slick fingers. The lock is Wanton's work, just like the steel bars across the door. The tech a gift from the company, although she expects they're paying for it, another budget line added to their debt, another pittance attached to the monumental sums they pay back by working in the heart of Downside's feral squalor.

Wanton's waiting for her when the door slides open.

Wanton in his camouflage gear, provided by the company at a generous discount. Wanton with his crew-cut and his broad, grinning face. Wanton with his massive fists, designed for blunt-force trauma. Wanton with his chest like an adult silverback, wide and thick with muscle. Cody figures they grafted a little gorilla DNA there, inserted it into the embryo just to get the soldier they wanted. Wanton glares at her, thick arms folded over that chest. "You're cutting it close," he says.

Cody nods, heading for the bathroom. Wanton trails behind her. "Job comes from Bellamy. Figured you'd want some warning."

"Ugh," she says, and it's enough. She doesn't have more, right now.

"The briefing may require actual words, yeah?" Wanton stands at the bathroom door, arms folded across the massive chest. The floorboards creak beneath him as he waits, patiently, for her to splash cold water over her face and swallow a fistful of painkillers. One pill for the nausea, another for the headache. A third, laced with nanites that mimic liver function, speeding her through the left-over booze that's burning a hole in her gullet. She sips water from the tap, figures the artificial bacteria the company injects every six weeks will take care of most infections. Then she hauls the bathroom door open, fixes Wanton with her sweetest smile. "Better?"

"Better would be a partner who follows protocol and orders."

"Orders are for soldiers." Cody heads to her bunk, selects another shirt from the neatly folded pile. "Soldiers work for the good of the people, not a fucking corp. We do this for the money, yeah?"

Wanton glares. He doesn't like that. Doesn't like hearing anything about the debt, all the shit they owe the company for the cost of defrost and decanting.

"What?" Cody says.

"I'm not a mercenary."

"No," she says. "Of course not."

Wanton turns away, lets her get dressed in peace. She grins at his retreating back, shucks herself free of the sweat-stained clothing. Shimmies into the fresh shirt. Fresh pants. Heavy boots, and an armoured vest. Corp supplied, all of it, hard enough to turn aside most knives. Good enough for field work, this side of the river. Wanton nods when she emerges, checks his watch and nods again. "Minute and a half to spare," he says. "Bellamy will be pleased."

"I couldn't give a shit," Cody says.

"And yet you're here, waiting for his call. Like a good dog." Wanton still has his back to her.

"You trying to be an asshole today?"

For a moment she thinks Wanton's going to yell, going to vent his frustrations for that crack about the merc. Instead, he grins at her. "Should have brought me breakfast. Whatever shit they spiked on those skewers smelled pretty good, you know?"

He punches Cody's shoulder, all friendly and shit, but it's still hard enough to register. A spike of pain flares through the peaceful sheath of the meds, reminds her there's still a few parts of a hangover that modern medicine can mask completely.

Cody hates it when Wanton tries to force camaraderie, make her feel like a friend instead of a partner. He's not bothered by the world outside their front door, full of Rat Boys and Crow Boys and the hulking brutes who join up with the Rampage; the zealous motherfuckers from the Evangelical White and the well-dressed, sack-masked kids who make up the Scarecrow Dandies. All those gangs fighting for territory, going to war over Cityside's scraps. Ever since they cracked Wanton out of cryo, he's been all kinds of loyal the company doesn't deserve.

Downside doesn't bother him. He doesn't know much else.

Cody, she knows better and it makes her hate everything. She hates the gangs and the squat and being on call. Hates the fact she can't go home, back to Cityside. That she's stuck here, in Downside, until Bellamy says otherwise and says her those three, sweet words she never expects to hear.

The call comes through at 13:00, right on goddamn schedule. Lucas Bellamy's face fills the screen, lean and quietly handsome, dark hair slicked back away from his face; his suit costing more than Cody's yearly retainer.

He smiles, leans closer to the camera. "Good to see you're both ready. It's going to be a day," he says. "We got reports one of the local gangs has uncovered some Sleeping Beauties. We'd like you to track 'em down, give coordinates to a recovery team."

Wanton's breath catches and his fingers tighten against the arm-rests of his chair. Cody just nods, remembers to be professional. "How much?"

Bellamy gives her a number. It's higher than expected.

"Alright," she says. "We're on it. Send through what you've got."

They both hate the mission, but this is the job. Bellamy handles defrost and decant, finds the Company its workforce. It costs a lot, to wake a sleeper. A hell of a lot, for the older jobs, back before cryosleep was common and they'd worked out how to do it safe. Plenty of those decanted end up on the same track, trawling Downside for other sleepers, paying down their debt; trying not to think about what happens once the job is done, or what happens to the decanted who don't have the skills for mercenary work. They just do the job, watch the debt go down. Dream about the day they're finally cut loose.

They let Bellamy talk through all the stuff the Company wants 'em to know, pretend like its useful intel. Truth is, Bellamy can't offer them shit. He's tucked away, safe and sound, in a com-ops room on Cityside, far from the sweaty heat and the streets full of gene-freak weirdos. He's reading back notes fed into his computer, adding details from satellite imaging and data scraped off the net. Treating it like it's military, like they're a couple of soldiers.

Truth is, that shit ain't useful, not for the job they've been given.

They gear up, once the call ends. Go in search of intelligence that won't get them killed, working their way through the brokers and dealers who know what's really going on.

Mackie Pelican, down near the tunnel, gives them the beginning of a story: turf wars between the Rampage and some rogue Evangelical-Whites, shit moved out of a warehouse under the cover of darkness. No guarantee it's sleepers, but the odds are better than most. The Ev-White like their cryo victims, like to indoctrinate while the newly wakened are groggy, slip 'em a few hits of Rapture to make sure the conversion sticks.

After that, they hit the second Valhalla Bar, check in with this skinny runt of a Corvidae by the name of Odin8. He tells them about a fight where the Rampage got stomped, six of the big boys ripped apart by three dozen Ev-White with two-handed swords. Way he hears it, Odin8's putting money on the Rampage getting payback, storming into the Ev-White territory and going at it, full-Kaiju, until there's nothing left but rubble.

From there, they hit the Floating Market, let Wanton talk to his own. Cody rides shotgun, ignores the discordant buzz of voices and the unsteady lurch of the boats beneath them. Wanton walks through the flotilla like he's born to it, even if this version of the market built up a good decade after he was first preserved in cryo. He smiles a little easier, out on the floating market, among folk who can speak his full name without stumbling and don't name him after food.

He learns more, too. Finds this little punk named Jun who tells 'em one of the Ev-White Pious is putting the call out for her paladins, gathering all swords to the Church of Razors deep in the heart of Ev-White turf. Consolidating the churches, building a small army. Bad news for everyone, Cody figures, 'specially the Rampage.

No-one likes the Evangelical Whites. Not the Rampage, not the Rat-Boys, not the Scarecrow Dandies. Not even the Corvidae, who chew avian-sequenced gene-morphs like they're some kind of goddamn candy and welcome the dangerously psychotic into their fucked-up family. These days the Ev-White are everywhere; white robes, white hair, white skin; a mad hate for the genetically-modified and a prayer on their lips. Crosses tattooed into their skulls and big, fuck-off swords held in a bloody grip.

The Evangelical White don't *believe* in a higher power; they take so much Rapture they're *sure* which gods exist, and they ain't afraid to tell you it's time to take their words as gospel.

Cody figures they can use that, once they've got confirmation the Beauties are in the Ev-White's possession. All they gotta do is talk to a primary source; separate the rumour from the real. She says as much to Wanton, and he scowls at her.

"We ain't going to The Slaughterhouse. Tell me you ain't that stupid."

"When ain't we that stupid," Cody says. "'Less you want to go fuck with the White, when we don't really have to."

He screws up his face, thinking that over. Knows that he's already lost this fight, and the night is going to get nasty.

·   ·   ·

She leads Wanton down to the river, takes point as they thread through the rusting husks of old cars left to decay on the shore. The river stinks, this time of the afternoon; the dark sludge of sewerage and chemical run-off baked into a fugue by 12 hours of daylight. Cody listens to the scuff of Wanton's boots, keeps her breathing shallow; swings underneath the old bridge, through the slices of sunlight filtering through the gap where the roadway should have been; hears gunfire in the distance, over on the far shore – the staccato song of Cityside water patrol, discouraging any attempt to cross the river. She ignores it. Heads for Slaughterhouse Bar. Knocks three times on the old iron door set into the redbrick wall.

The hinges protest when Naga finally answers, one hand held up to fend off the orange light. He's old, for a Rampage. Near blind in daylight, even if his night-vision is good. Still big, still dangerous, with shoulders that brush against the doorway and steel teeth like the fangs of a snake. Grafted scales cover his face and his nostrils flare as he sniffs, scenting the air like a half-mad dog, eager to pick a fight. Wanton reaches for his pistol, but Cody grabs his arm.

"Nag'," she says. "Been a while, eh?"

He eases, a little, at the sound of her voice. Lays one hand against the door to keep himself steady, reaches out with the other to touch Cody's face. Wanton growls a little, but Cody shushes him. Keeps her focus on the half-blind giant trying to feel the contours of her cheek. "Jones?" he says. "Shit, babe. You can't be here."

She takes hold of his blunt fingers, pushes them away. "Wish we had a choice in that. Unfortunately, we don't."

Naga blinks into the sunset. "Always got a choice, babe."

"Not today," she says. "Today we got a job. Heard some rumours about the Rampage, figured we might have a chat to the Kong, yeah? See if he knows what's what?"

Naga sucks on his fangs a moment. "You got that big fucker with ya?"

"Yeah, I got him."

"You know what it'll take, getting the Kong onside?"

She looks back at Wanton. "Yeah, we know."

Naga lets out a short, barking laugh. Shuffles back into the darkness. "Best you come in then," he says. "We'll see what can be done."

The temperature drops the moment they cross the threshold. The inside of the Slaughterhouse lives up to the name: wrecked tables, wrecked chairs, wrecked walls, refrigeration unites jacked up hard because the Rampage run so hot. Steel hooks dangle from the ceiling, where the Rampage hang the losers after a brawl. Bloodstains on the concrete, benches and tables made of stone. Hard enough to survive a fight between men who jack up on rhino DNA after they hit the limits of traditional steroid enhancement.

The sour stink of old sweat and blood wages war with the river stench. Naga limps over to the bar, grabs a bottle of piss-yellow booze from the shelf and pours a trio of drinks. He knocks one back, pushes the second Cody's way.

Wanton ignores the third, focused on the hallway leading into the freezers. Naga scowls, drinks it for him, his eyes a little better away from the daylight. "Well," he says, "why d'ya need the Kong?"

Cody toys with her shot-glass. "We got some questions about salvage his boys found."

"Boys find a lot of salvage." Naga pours another round of drinks.

"This happened a few days back."

The second shot disappears into Naga's considerable gullet. "Not sure he'll remember."

"He'll remember," Wanton says in a cold, neat voice. He stands away from the bar, makes sure he's got room to move. Probably a smart call, given the way their last visit played out.

Naga doesn't say anything.

Wanton doesn't say shit, either.

"Christ, Nag', just get him," Cody says, "or it's me who'll kick your ass."

Naga blinks, a little amused by that. He may be old, but he's still hard. Hard enough that the Rampage don't kick him out, when they live to break the weak. He reaches for the intercom, holds his thumb against it. "Visitors," he says, when someone finally answers. "Two of 'em, corporate. Let him know they'd like to talk."

The Kong's entrance doesn't shake the room, but he's big enough it should. Three more Rampage trail along behind him, a good head shorter than their boss's massive bulk. The Kong is all muscle and scales, ridges of bone grafted to his skull. An ugly lump of rage with some extra rage heaped on. He lugs a haunch of meat, lips stained with the juice. The fingers wrapped around the bone are steel chords, his teeth like the blades of a thresher. Bare chest covered in scar tissue that score his dark flesh like a series of hashtag. One of those scars is Cody's work. Another – the biggest of them – he got from his last clash with Wanton. The Kong glares, attention focused on her partner. He points his haunch of meat. Says, "Well, well. The big man."

Wanton drops a hand to the knife sheathed at his belt. "Lord Kong," he says. "You're upright."

"I heal fast, big man. Learn from my mistakes." The Kong slaps his chest three times, each one loud as a gunshot. "You ready for a rematch, Wanton? Want to show me how strong you are?"

Wanton shrugs. "Business first. Fun later."

The Kong leans forward, heavy knuckles ground the granite bar. "Business," he says. "Alright. Let's pretend we got business, then, 'fore I rip off your arm."

Cody steps between them, pushes up with her toes to

make sure she breaks the Kong's hard stare. "Take the left arm," she says. "He shoots right-handed."

The ponderous head drops down to regard her. "Ain't concerned with his shooting anyone, girl."

"You're not, I am." Cody meets the slitted yellow eyes inherited from some serpent. "We ain't here to rumble, Kong. Just looking for information."

The Kong shows his teeth, all shards of gleaming steel. "Ain't got nothing for you, Miss Jones."

"Really? That's surprising. We heard you lost some boys to the Ev-White last night. Heard they came after you, on your own turf, so they could make off with some shit you found."

The Kong's eyes narrow. He turns and glares at Naga. "You hear a lot."

"I have good ears. It comes from avoiding the kinds of body-mods that'll turn me into a lizard."

"Ears can be ripped off." The Kong say it cold and angry, but she knows that's just a front. Naga is still in the room, watching the exchange. Naga who used to be Kong, way back, before he stepped aside to let a stronger man take charge. Weakness can be fatal, when your crew worship strength.

Cody lets the Kong straighten up, lets him come round the table and loom a little. Lets him have his moment, before he looks down at the pistol she's pointing at his knee. "You can take out an ear," she says, "but I can blow out your knee. Nothing glamorous 'bout hobbling round with a slug in your leg, Kong. Sure as hell not going to help you when Wanton starts getting nasty."

She holds his stare, smiles at him. "Of course, we choose not to do that, 'cause it would be impolite, but the option is always there. It's good to have options, yeah?"

The Kong snarls, but he backs off. "Like the big man better," he says. "He don't fight dirty, Jones."

"I'm at peace with being the lesser option." She shrugs, raises the gun. "So, we going to be reasonable 'bout this?"

"Reasonable ain't our way."

"Adapt," Cody says. "You're missing a few boys?"

"I'm not—"

She puts a bullet into the floor, right by his feet. The Kong doesn't flinch, neither does Naga. Both of them, hard as concrete.

"Alright," The Kong says. "My missing boys got worked over by the Ev-White. Three of my best, all dead now."

"And what were your best doing, when they got cut apart?"

"Like I know," The Kong says. "Ain't like we're Ratboys, living in each other's pockets."

Wanton's boots scuff the concrete. He advances, gets in The Kong's face. "You're full of shit," he says. "You may be a pack of Mastodons, but you're still a damn pack. Ain't none of your boys doing shit worth getting killed for, not without you knowing."

The Kong rips a hunk of meet off the bone, glares at Wanton while he chews.

"Mastodons," he says, "I like that."

And Cody sees the twitch at the corner of his mouth, recognises the intent in his tone. The cold invitation to brawl, one on one, with the only other male big enough to make a fight of it. The Kong rises and discards the meat, wipes his ham-hock fingers against his bare chest. The greasy smear highlights the scars. It ain't like The Kong is a pushover. He's tough as boiled leather and built like a tank, keeps coming regardless of the injury. Makes it easy to forget that he's smart, underneath the attitude and testosterone.

He goes nose-to-nose with Wanton. Smirks as the two of them stare at each other. "You wanna know 'bout my boys," he says, "you gotta fight me for it. Draw blood, I answer your questions."

"An' if you bleed me?" Wanton doesn't make it sound like a potential option, just something he wants to know.

The Kong jerks his head at Cody. "We move on to the bonus round, and I try to take her ear," he says. "Owe both of you scars, one way or another. Been meaning to—"

Wanton snaps his forehead into The Kong's nose. Bunches a giant fist and smashes it into a scale-covered throat, leaves The Kong gasping and struggling for air. Neat work against a normal man, designed to incapacitate, but the Rampage are built tough.

The Kong wraps his arms round Wanton, drives his back into the stone edge of a bar. Naga shuffles forward, ready to help out. Cody intercepts him, holds an arm against his chest. "Leave it," she says, and Naga nods. Survival of the fittest here.

That's good. It means Cody doesn't have to shoot him, and piss of the one ally they still have in giant country.

The two behemoths stay locked together, struggling for leverage. Wanton gets it first, puts The Kong down. Punches him in the face until he sees blood. Holds the bloodied fist in The Kong's eye line. "We done?"

The Kong glares. Spits blood. "Done," he rasps, his throat still raw. "Get off me."

Wanton sits back, wipes sweat off his face. Tries to hide the fact that his hand is hurting. Trying not to show weakness, not while Naga and the other Rampage are watching.

Cody takes his place, crouches down beside The Kong. "So," she says, "your boys?"

The Kong pushes her away, struggles to his feet. "Follow Nag, he'll show ya."


It's still cold down in the bunker. White tiles streaked with rime, a think sheet of mist clinging to the ground. Cody hugs herself to keep warm, follows Wanton in. Blue lights on the ceiling keep everything just this side of visible, hurts her eyes. There's blood splatter on the walls, obvious signs of a fight. Three corpses in the centre of the room, all of them big and deceased for days. The walls hum, the ancient tubing that kept the cryonics active struggle to keep working now the glass coffins have been opened. Eight cryo-tubes are pressed up against the wall. Seven of them are empty now, their doors open and coughing out plumes of cryoprotectants.

Naga lingers by the door, refusing to come in. Leaves Cody and Wanton to poke through, piecing together what happened. They're two stories down, underneath an old church on the fringe of Rampage turf. Cody figures it for a black-market facility, from the days before preservation became commonplace.

She eyes the open doorways, does the math. Seven sleepers are worth good money, if you can get 'em across the river. They're citizens of another time, desperate people who trusted technology to catch up with 'em one day. Figured they'd hit the future and someone would thaw 'em out, reverse the effects of cryogenesis without damaging the grey matter.

In truth, they got it half right. The Company loves the sleepers, for all sorts of reasons. Some get used as human subjects, when there's no official records to make it complicated. Some get decanted and put to work, paying off the debt incurred by the process. The rest? She tries not to think about it. That's how she sleeps at night.

Wanton examines the tech. "Vintage stuff," he says. "Very old-school. Poor bastards are lucky the generators lasted."

Naga coughs, from his place by the door. "Not so lucky if the Ev-White got 'em."

"No," Wanton says. He gives Cody a look. She ignores him, heads for the eighth tube. It's an archaic design, steel and thick glass, red light blinking at the bottom of the casing. She rubs her sleeve against the glass. The cold bites into her arm like it's a savage, desperate animal.

The girl inside is withered, mummified by the cold, lips thin and blue. Killed when the sealant on her tube deteriorated, letting the body freeze instead of keeping it preserved, ice crystals forming and destroying the cells. "You sure all the others were alive?"

Naga's lips peel away from the snake fangs. "Would you two be here, otherwise?"

She lets that go. Steps aside to give Wanton access to the corpse. He knows more about Cryo than she ever will, learned all the details before his own cold sleep. Part of his training, way back when. Nothing like her own experience.

She's asked him about it in the past. Wanton didn't say much, just told her he's thankful he didn't end up a husk. That he came out with a chance to do right by the Company.

Almost made it sound sincere, which is why they like him better. Wanton can fake compliance far better than Cody can.

He gets quiet, as he looks over the dead girl. Cody knows just how he feels, wheels around to glare at Naga. "You should have called us," she says, "the moment your boys found this place. We could have paid you a fair price, kept your busy from getting cut up"

Naga's eyes narrow. "You two ain't the only popsicles working this patch of turf."

"Ain't talking about the company," she says. "You should have called *us*."

Naga tilts his head, lips hooked into a crude smile. "The Kong made a call. Figured he'd get more, letting people bid."

She nudges one of the dead Rampage with the toe of her boot. "How's that working out for ya?"

Naga doesn't answer. She doesn't really blame him. If they're looking for confirmation, the three corpses do the job. Swords leave distinctive wounds, 'specially when there's lots of 'em, and in Downside it's the Ev-White who have a monopoly on that kind of violence. She crouches, takes a closer look at the stab wounds on a corpse.

The Ev-White work ugly, hacking at their victim, but they get all kinds of delicate once they've put a man down. Little cruciforms carved into their victims, to aid passage to the afterlife. A good wound could tell her which sect took the bodies, narrow down which Pious they've got to hassle on the Street of Churches. This one is messy work, 'cause the Rampage are hard to carve. Too much thick skin and muscle. Too many scales to work around.

"Would have thought you boys were too careful to let the Ev-White know 'bout this," she says. "Had to know they'd come recruiting, if they heard tell of the sleepers."

Naga snorted. "The Kong got careless."

"He put guards here."

"Three guards ain't a lot," Naga says.

"Can't think of anyone that'll tangle with three Rampage willingly."

"Except the Evangelical White." Naga shakes his thick head. "Mongo—" he points to the closest dead Rampage "—he was going to be Kong, one day. Smart kid. Strong. Stupid, him going down like this."

"Not many smart ways to die, mate." Wanton looks up from the dead girl. "We got what we need?"

Cody nods. "You healthy enough for a run at the White? The Kong put a beating on ya."

Wanton shrugs. "I'll manage."

"We can head back to the base, give you a few hours to heal up, you know?"

Wanton thumbs his tablet, shows her a page of data. "Computers are old enough that the encryption ain't shit," he says. "Skimmed all data. According to what we got here, the Ev-White prepped 'em for defrost."

Cody looks around, takes in the ancient tech. "These guys?"

Wanton nods.

"How in hell they managing that?"

"Poorly, is my guess," Wanton says. "Figure we've got an hour, maybe a little longer, before there's no chance of decanting 'em safe."

He sets a stopwatch on his handheld, and tucks it away at his belt.

"Shit," Cody says.

"Yeah." Wanton nods. "That's about the size of it."

They head home, gear up: shotguns, spare ammo, more body-armour. Part of the gig, this side of the river, is avoiding a show of force. Letting the fragile ecosystem of thugs and gangs do its thing, maintain the status quo. Let everyone think they're corporate mercs, not soldiers on a payroll. But screw that, when you're heading into Ev-White turf, home of sword-wielding maniacs with the power of faith behind 'em. Home to churches devoted to mixing up Rapture, each hit designed to let you see God, or Gods, or Goddesses. Eliminating any doubt, until faith becomes certain knowledge.

The Evangelical White took over the cliffs by the river, built the Street of Churches looking towards the far bank and the city. Bonfires in the evenings, letting Cityside know they're there. Loud, moaning group prayers as the faithful maintain their vigil. And everywhere, Paladins, the most faithful of the faithful. Men and women in pristine robes, sodium-white hair left to grow long and wild. Yellow cruciforms tattooed onto their foreheads, daubed with neon face-paint that lights up like rays of the sun.

Cody takes point as they walk along the river bank and turn left onto the Street of Churches. Everyone looks the same on the street: same hair, same robes, the same wild-eyed beatitude that comes from too many drugs. So the Ev-White look, as she strolls down the Street with Wanton, everyone aware there's outsiders in their midst. Wanton unholsters his shotgun, keeps it handy to discourage the onlookers from making an unwanted conversation.

They pass the Church of Razors, daubed with blood and viscera. The Paladin's out front sneering at them with red-stained lips, spoiling for bloodshed.

They pass Last Pure Church and the two men standing guard have skin the same shade as their hair. They eye Wanton, eye the shotgun. Whisper among themselves, looking for a fight.

They pass the Forgotten Church, little more than an empty lot amid the close-press of buildings, a place for new preachers to unleash fire-and-brimstone sermons among the poor and the forgotten that wash up on the street. The lot stinks of sweaty flesh and bleach, lines of newcomers crouched by plastic bowls, dying their hair to fit in. Up the back of the lot, perched on a stone, one of the Pious is working. He looks up when they walk past, turns his eye towards the heavens. "Interlopers," he moans, "unfaithful."

"Like we fuckin' care,'"Cody says, moving on, ducking into the shadows.

They head to the First Great Church of the White, the sole building that started out as a place of worship. Wide expanses of marble, trimmed in gold. Dead fountains, in the courtyard, flanking a small angel statue. The place where the Paladin's gather, waiting for their orders.

The home of Pious Demeter, the source of all Rapture, who welcomed in the sick and the homeless, who gave them a place to exist. Demeter who preaches against the gene-grafts and body-mods that make the other gangs distinct, tells the faithful that they must stay pure if they want to get another hit.

Demeter, who made the Ev-White possible, who keeps

them running through drugs and intimidation as much as her own damn cunning.

The courtyard is big, lots of stairs and marble. Thirty meters to the building, two short sets of stairs as you follow the rise of the hill. Paladins camped out, armed and half-mad with Rapture. Cody figures there's twenty of 'em, maybe twenty-five. Another thirty Ev-White, no signs of a blade, but that doesn't mean much once a fight starts. A bell-tower in the church itself, the bell long-removed and replaced by spotlights. Two men in the tower, both armed with crossbows, keeping a look out. Archaic tech, but it'll do the job. The snipers are both trained, know how to shoot. The fence is steel bars, hard to climb, easy to see through. But getting in without being noticed takes time, planning, and they're running short on both.

The smart move would be letting it go, pretending the job ain't worth it.

No chance they can do the smart thing either, so they're going to play this dumb.

The Honourable Hades sees them coming, separates himself from the pack. Old, for a paladin, his white thatch of hair receding, his face scored with creases worn into to the flesh. He knows them both, 'cause that's his job. Knows everyone in Downside who presents a danger to the White. His eyes are wild, pupils the size of pinpricks. He sways, blocking the gate, eyes shifting from Cody to Wanton. "The Church is closed to visitors," he bellows. "Demeter cannot meet with you today."

Most days, they'd try to talk their way in, play upon the fact that Hades doesn't really want a fight. He's nervous about the shotguns, nervous about Wanton's strength, nervous about the gear the Company's provided to make a team like Wanton and Cody more dangerous than any two men in his crew.

Most days they'd try to talk their way in, but Wanton's ten types of pissed right now; focused on the mission and the ticking clock. He looks to Cody, gives her a nod. Pulls the trigger on the shotgun. The sound of it spills across the empty courtyard, puts a slug deep into the meat of Honourable Hades' arm. Cody swears and throws smoke, yellow canisters tumbling across the courtyard and belching up their contents. Wanton doesn't hesitate, dives into the billowing cloud with the shotgun pressed tight to his shoulder. Cody gets her pistols out, follows close behind. Honourable Hades' runs, screams orders as he retreats. His voice is drowned in the frightened shouts of half-blind, rapturous Paladins looking for a target.

Crossbows fire, up in the guard tower, bolts whistling through the air. The first instinct is to flinch and duck for cover, but Cody trusts the smoke to keep her safe. The bolts hit the concrete by the gate, well short of their position. Cody keeps moving, following the dark silhouette of Wanton's bulk. He moves fast, shotgun booming as he clears a path. She follows behind, her pistols the precision against the wide-scatter blast of Wanton's gun. She double-taps a Paladin who comes charging through the smoke. Double-taps another who stumbles close, sword raised and his eyes watering.

They hit the first stairs at a run, take them two at a time. The Paladins are everywhere, bellowing warnings, screams, and orders. The other Ev-White are no better, milling in a panic. One of them leaps at Wanton, trying to drag him down. Wanton swings the shotgun stock, connects with the right cheek. Bones break. Blood splatters the concrete. Creates an opening for a Paladin who lumbers in, swinging his sword. The metal bites a chunk out of Wanton's leg, blood soaking the marble. Wanton swears, plants a boot in the Paladin's guts, kicks him free to buy some space. Cody follows up, puts two into the Paladin's chest, forgets him as they move on.

Another set of stairs. Three meters to the front door. The Honourable Hades reaches it first, heads in and slams the doors behind him. Wanton moves like a wrecking ball, smashing through all opposition. He applies his shoulder to the seam between the doors, before they're properly shut. Cody drops another canister, leaves the smoke to cover their entrance. Kicks the doors closed, once they're through, and slams a bar down to lock them.

The long hall stretches out in front of them, lined with ancient pews. Hades limps backwards, bleeding from his bullet wounds. He's got his sword drawn and ready, holds it like a barricade that will keep Wanton from coming.

It doesn't. Wanton advances on him, doesn't even bother using the shotgun as a threat. Now it's just size, the relentless rejection of pain. Hades swings and Wanton jerks sideways, comes back with a punch that sends Hades sprawling. The sword skitters away, disappearing under the pews. "Sleepers," Wanton snarls. "We know your crew took 'em."

"Unbeliever! Foul beast of—"

Wanton jams his shotgun against Hades' spleen. "Losing patience, man."

The Paladin spits. Wanton doesn't like that. A big boot stomps The Honourable Hades' face, busts open that leathery skin. Rears back for another shot, but Cody grabs his arm. Hauls him back, before he breaks Hades' skull, leave them with a whole church to go through and no real clues where to start.

Hades grins. Knows what he's doing. Paladins thump on the barricaded door. Feet hammer the marble down the sides of the church, his men scrambling for another way in. Kill enough time and they'll be outnumbered, trapped in the close confines of the Church, nowhere to run.

The bell-tower door swings open: the sniper from up top.

He bursts into the room, like he's expecting an easy fight. Hesitates, when he sees there's no other Ev-White around.

Cody drops him. Two to the chest. She kneels beside Hades, holsters the gun. "That shit you're on," she says. "I know what it does. No pain, no fear. I get that. Means my friend can beat on you and there's no reason to tell us nothing, so I ain't going to bother with hurting ya."

"Bride of—"

"Yeah, I get it. Genetic abomination. Creature of the devils and the nine hells and all that." She produces a syringe, lets him have a good look at the stainless-steel tip. "Thing is, I don't give a shit 'bout any of that, but your lot certainly do. And I figure that shit Demeter cooks up, it's gotta have one hell of a come-down, yeah?"

She jams the needle into his arm.

"Borrowed that from a friend of mine, one of the Corvidae. Enough gene-morphs to turn Wanton into a fucking crow-boy, let alone a scrawny runt like you. Won't hurt too much, but it won't be all that pleasant."

Hades writhes, trying to break free. Fear in his eyes now, behind the chemically-induced bravado. Wanton plants a boot on Hades' chest, holds him in place. Cody brushes Hades' bloody forehead. She puts her thumb against the plunger. "Shh," she says. "You know it won't hurt."

He doesn't talk. He won't talk, even with that threat hanging over him. But his eyes flick towards the small door at the rear, tucked in behind the altar. She presses down, injects him. Waits the few seconds it takes for the needle to do its work.

Wanton takes his foot off the body. Raises his shaggy eyebrows. "Never seen a mutagen that knocks a guy out."

"Morphine," she says.

Wanton shakes his head.

"Gene-morphs are stupid expensive," Cody says. "And we owe enough already."

The door leads down, into the basement level. Overhead lights powered by solar batteries, a little gasp of cold air that causes their skin to dimple. Cody thumbs her headset, puts a call through to the company.

They answer and Fredrick Bellamy's voice oozes into her ear. "Miss Jones, good to hear from you. I take it you have something for me?"

"Sure," she lies. "Send in an extraction team. Centre in on our coordinates."

"Excellent," Bellamy says. "Team will be there in five."

Wanton is resting his bulk against the pew, keeping his weight off the leg. "Calling in the cavalry?" he says. "That'll get expensive, if we've got this wrong"

"We still got five minutes," she says. "Figure that's enough to search this shit-hole, even with your leg to slow us down."


The underground level is where the Rapture happens, little black-market labs where Demeter mixes up her drug. They find a handful of white-robed assistants, clear them out without much effort. Find Demeter herself, way up the back, hiding among the glass-fronted coffins stolen from the bunker. Coffins sweating moisture as they warm, dark puddles on the concrete. Demeter half-crouched, too tall for the low bench to provide any cover.

Wanton flies across the room, pins her against the wall with his shotgun barrel. Demeter throws useless punches at Wanton's face, trying to break free. It's annoying, instead of effective. Wanton snarls and slams his forehead into Demeter's face, stuns her long enough to get her on the ground. He uses his weight to keep her there, knee in the centre of her back. Produces a zip-tie and secures her arms, then covers the entrance with his shotgun.

"We good?"

Cody crouches beside the first coffin, plugs in her tablet.

Checks the readings: dropping temperature; blood filtration; a lot of familiar drugs. Some of them pharmaceutical, to keep the sleeper calm. Some of them nanotechnology, repairing any long-term damage 'caused by the decades sleeping. It's slick, professional work. Expensive as hell, just for one person, half the reason she and Wanton owe the company so damn much.

And Demeter's got seven popsicles, thawing out in her lab. "Selling god to junkies pays better than I thought," she says. "Jesus, Dem'. Where in hell'd you get all this?"

Demeter gurgles a response that could be laughter. Wanton raises his knee, glances in Cody's direction. "All what?" he says.

"She's got a full thaw happening. Everything that's needed, right here on the premises."

"The fuck?" Wanton reaches down, grabs Demeter by the throat. Drags her over with one hand, so he can take a closer look. Demeter's laughing for real, now that she can breathe.

"The Gods work in mysterious ways," she says.

"Not that goddamn mysterious." Wanton drops her, trusts Cody to keep her out of trouble. Picks up the tablet and scans the details, brow creased, fingers scrolling from screen to screen. He grunts, once he's done with it all. Unplugs the tablet and moves to the next goddamn coffin. "This ain't right," he says. "No way the Ev-White can pull this off."

"We do this for holy glory," Demeter intones, like she's preaching to the faithful. "We do this here, where we can be seen, so that all shall know—"

Cody slaps her. "Shut up," she says. "If the next words out of your mouth aren't 'this is how we did this,' he's going to be pissed and I won't stop him."

"Does the how of it really matter? It's done. That's what's important."

"No," Wanton says. "Cody, if these readings—"

"That isn't the job," Cody says, and she hates herself for saying it.

"Screw the job," Wanton says. "If they can wake up out here, without the Company's help–"

"The companies already coming. No way can we smuggle seven coffins out on the sly, not before Bellamy gets his crew in here."

Wanton closes his eyes a moment, takes a long breath through his nose. He lumbers over on his bad leg, hauls Pious Demeter upright. "Answers," he says. "Tell me how?"

"A gift." Demeter's grin is crimson and she's forced to spit blood. "Even a gene-beast may learn the error of his ways, and do his best to secure the help of an angel."

'"he fuck?" Wanton turns to Cody, ready to plead. Ready to ask her if she'd please just screw the debt, do this one thing and help him get the coffins out. Help him make sense of the shit Demeter's talking, if it's even possible to make sense out of all that.

But there's a commotion down the hall, up the stairs, up on the surface. The groan of the drop-ship coming down. Gas canisters, gunfire, *go-go-go*. The symphony of the retrieval team securing the landing zone, coming through the building. Fredrick Bellamy and a team of loyal company soldiers, here to take out the cargo and deliver them to the corporate office for processing.

Even if she'd been willing to say yes, their window for getting the sleeping beauty's out is officially closed and done.

The drop-ship lifts off, tubes safely stowed. Three members of the extraction team bleeding, waiting for the medic to finish checking the Beauties vital signs. Bellamy sits in the seat by the door, shit-eating grin in place. He beams at her, beams at Wanton, keeps telling 'em they did good. Cody doesn't feel it. No adrenaline left, for starters, which means the aches are starting. The dull burn along her arm where a blade got too close, the bruises and scrapes that didn't register as they got the job done. Wanton looks worse, all beat-to-hell and bleeding, unwilling to accept treatment from the medic before he knows how the defrost is going.

Cody figures what she really wants is series of cold drinks, followed by hangover pain that's well and truly all her fault. It's better that way, she thinks, having someone to blame. Makes her think, one day, she can change all this. Leave the pain behind.

"They going to be okay?" Codys asks, and Wanton doesn't answer. She glances over to Bellamy, who does that little, beneficent half-nod that makes her want to punch him.

"Listen," Bellamy says, and his smile disappears. So she listens. Focuses her scowl on him, makes it clear she doesn't want to be doing this. Wanton is still distracted, looking over his shoulder at the Sleeper's pods. Still dripping blood onto the metal floor, the cloth pressed against the wound in his thigh doing fuck-all to stop the bleeding.

"Listen," Bellamy says, "we can't take you back over the river. You both know that, right? You've got facilities, in the safe-house. Enough to patch yourselves up and heal? You don't need us to ship anything else over to you?"

He nods at Wanton, like he actually gives a damn. Cody feels ready to crack up and laugh, but she holds it together. Nods.

"Yeah," she says, "we're good. Get us clear and drop us by the river, we can make our way back from there."

"And the trouble with the White?" Bellamy's pushing, pretending too are.

"We got it covered," Wanton says. His voice so cold and even it reminds Cody of well-made knife.

"Great." Cody's smile is back again. White teeth. Thin, bloodless lips. "So great to have team players on board Great job down there, on the ground. You've got a bonus coming. I'll put in the paperwork, once we get back. Just—"

"Bellamy?"

His perfectly manicured eyebrows rise, and she wonders how long it's been since someone interrupted him. Cody shakes her head, appalled. Doesn't bother hiding it.

"Shut up," she says. "We don't actually give a damn."

"But the money," he says. "Buying out of your contract?"

"We both know that's never happening." She nods her head at Wanton, still watching the medic work. "We're out here for the long haul, me and him both. We know the deal, and how we're being screwed, and we're playing by the rules. Don't try and shit in our mouths, and we'll do the damn jobs you want done."

Bellamy's eyes narrow, like he's trying to figure that out. "Okay," he says, "no shit."

"That's all I ask," Cody says. She thumps Wanton in the shoulder. "You good to go, big guy?"

He grunts, and she takes it as yes. It's more than he's said since take-off.

The drop-ship angles left, swings towards the bridge. "By the way," Bellamy says, "I've got another gig for you. Quick one, but solid money. Enough to drop a few days off your debt." He reaches under his chair, produces a black case. Pushes it into Cody's hands and nods at her, encouragingly. "Drop that off at the Slaughterhouse, for your friend Kong. It's the money corporate owes him, for the finder's fee."

Cody scowls at the money. "You dealt with The Kong directly?"

"Nah, one of his flunkies called. Old bloke. Spoke on Kong's behalf."

Right, Cody thinks. She holds the case in a tight, white-knuckle grip. "Alright," she says. "Delivery."


The Slaughterhouse is empty. No meat, no bar, just hooks, concrete, and steel. The coppery stink of drying blood, an old smell that's never coming out. Wanton follows her in, pulls one of the hooks from the ceiling. Tests it with the flesh of his thumb. "You reckon they all cleared outta here?"

"I reckon there's been a coup." Cody heads for the meat lockers, pistol already drawn. She holds it low, keeps the case in her other hand. Moves slow and quiet as she approaches the steel doors. She can hear someone groaning, deep in the darkness. Wanton produces a flashlight, shines it over her shoulder. They go three doors down, slide the locker open.

The Kong, lying on the floor. Blood seeping through the wound in his stomach, intestines exposed to the world. Already so far gone he's ready for the water, just another ex-resident of Downside getting dumped into the river. "Damn," Cody says. "Kong, man, what the hell."

"Jones." He peers up at her, eyes little more than slits. His voice rasping out in a weak, trembling whisper. "Big man. Owe you some scars, eh?"

Wanton steps into the narrow locker, crouches down beside the dying man. "Good thing you heal fast, man. That one looks nasty."

"Ain't nothing." The Kong's voice is little more than a whisper. "Kick your ass, when I'm healed."

Cody bites her lower lip. It's not just the gut-wounds, although that's bad enough. It's the bruises, the signs of a beating. Lots of punches delivered by big men with a grudge, determined to do some damage. She considers the case, hanging from her left hand. "Thought this was for you," she says, "but I'm guessing you ain't The Kong anymore."

"Always said you were smart."

She turns, and Naga is standing in the doorway, big shoulders blocking the morning light. He isn't quite so hunched anymore, stands like a man who isn't in any pain. He watches her, no trouble seeing at night. Points to the case. "Pretty sure that's mine."

Cody raises the .45, holds it steady and trained on Naga's

chest. "Not the orders we were given," she says. "Don't get paid 'less it goes to the right man."

"Jones, please." A low smirk hooks the edge of Naga's mouth, made horrible by the teeth and the scales. "You and your friend, you're good at what you do, but you've never been known for stupidity. You've already fought one war, you don't need another." He steps aside, lets her see through the door. All the Rampage are gathered, lined up on the street outside. Watching, waiting, to see how this goes down. To see how the new Kong handles things.

"This isn't personal, it's politics," he says. "The Kong was weak. We needed someone strong."

"And you figured that was you?"

Again, the smirk. "I was qualified for the job. Stronger, smarter, more experience. Richer, too, once that case gets handed over."

"And if we don't?"

"Then I finish what the Ev-White started, grind your bones to dust." Naga shrugs, studies the steel talons attached to his fingers. "Not the option I'd prefer, given all you've done for me, but I'll take it. I need a show of strength. You can back down now, and give it to me, or I can make with the grinding. Either way, I get the victory."

Wanton snarls and launches himself across the room, steel hook in hand. He whips it through the air, steel point whistling, but Naga ducks back, gives ground, stays safe. He waits for an opening, drives his foot into the wounded leg with all the force his frame can manage. Wanton stumbles, teeth clenched in pain, and strong hands wrap around his wrist. Bones creak as Naga twists, forcing the hook from his hand. Looks up, meets Cody's stare. "Can't help but notice you didn't shoot me."

"Didn't want to hit my partner."

Naga grins and pushes Wanton over, plants a kick in the big man's ribs. "No chance of that now," he says, spreading his big arms wide. "I'll make it real easy for ya, Jones, but you know what it means when you leave."

"Yeah," she says, "I know." She puts the case on the floor, takes three steps away from it. Wanton stares at her, his face a bloody mess. Stares like he can't believe what she's doing.

Naga steps over him, heads for the case. Gets within three steps before Cody raises the pistol. "You set this up," she says. "That's why you left the others out there. Don't want them to know that you were paid to make it all possible. You told Demeter where to find the Sleepers. You fronted the cash she needed for seven defrosts, so hitting the bunker seemed like a good deal."

Naga doesn't raise his hands. Can't, when there's other Rampage watching. But he nods his head, just slightly. "You're a smart woman, Jones. Always liked that about you."

"Called in the tip to Bellamy 'cause you knew we'd come looking. Knew Wanton would beat down The Kong—"

"Ex-Kong," Naga says.

"Whatever. It doesn't matter. You played us, Nag'. That was smart. Right up until this point."

"Because your wrath will be swift and terrible?"

"'Cause it cost you a bundle to fund a full-thaw, and now you need that cash. And now you've got two witnesses who know exactly how all this went down, which means you have to kill us or find a way to keep us quiet."

"Killing you was always my preference."

"Harder than it looks," she says. "Paying us would be cheaper."

Naga glances back at Wanton. "You think I can't take that lump of meat?"

Cody holsters the gun. Shrugs off her jacket. "Wasn't thinking about him," she says. "You ever been beat by a woman, Nag? Can't imagine how that will go down with the boys."

Naga looks her over. "Ain't afraid to kill a woman, Jones."

"You seen the world out there, moron? Outside your little coven of overly mucho gene-twists, people ain't been afraid of killing women for a couple of hundred years."

Naga snarls, charges. Swipes at her with a giant paw. She grabs it, twists, uses his momentum to send him across the room. Up into the corner, away from the door. Far away from prying eyes.

He spins, ready for another charge. She doesn't give him a chance, gets up close with a combat knife and puts it in his stomach. "People think Wanton's the dangerous one," she says. "Truth is, he's just the nice one. He'll let you walk away from a fight. I'll force you to fucking crawl."

Naga snarls, but he buys it. Backs away a little, one hand over his gut.

"You really want to do this, Nag? Ain't going to go well for you."

Naga breathes heavy. Bunches his shoulders. She reverses her grip on the knife, drops down and waits for him to come closer.

He takes a step, winces at the pain in his guts. Looks at the shiny point of her blade. "Alright," he says. "The contents of the case?"

"That'll do for starters."

"Jones." Wanton stands, unsteady on his feet. "Jones, what—"

"Shut it," she says. "I said it'll do for starters. We take the money and we keep our mouths shut. Let everyone outside think you beat the Company. But you owe us, and not just money. For starters, we want a name."

The snake-faced moron blinks. "A name?"

"A name. Your contact who put it together, all the tech required for the defrost."

"But that's—"

"I can talk real loud," Cody says. "I can make a challenge every asshole out there will hear."

Naga nods. "Alright, the name. The name and the money. Deal?"

"For now," Cody says. "Wanton, get out of sight. Load the case with all the cash, then you and I are out of here."

"Cody—"

"Not a conversation. This is how it is."

She stares at him and he stares back, but she's not the one who looks away. Naga kneels down, collects the case. Takes it to the granite bar where his boys can't see, unloads the contents in neat, pretty stacks. Steps away so she can collect it, makes sure he stays out of arms reach.

Cody smacks herself in the face hard enough to break the skin. Grins through the bloody mess and points towards the door. "Over there. Look scary," she says. "Keep the case in hand."

Naga's jaw is tight as hell, but he does it without question. Stands over Wanton, case in both hands, ready to bludgeon him. Wanton rolls over, his face a bloody mess. "I give," he says, just loud enough for someone outside to hear.

For a moment, Naga teeters, ready to go through with it. Cody almost wonders if she'll have to kill the bastard.

Then he takes it. Lowers the case. Helps Wanton to his feet. Claps the big man on the shoulder, like it's just another victory. Keeps all the focus right on him while she collects the money.

She gets Wanton over one shoulder, steadies himself beneath his weight. Gets them out of there, while Naga's still celebrating. Gets some distance between them and the Slaughterhouse.

Wanton groans as she gets him staggering, steering him back towards home. "Money ain't going to be nothing," he says. "Ain't going to buy down the debt that much."

"Ain't for the debt," she says.

"Yeah?"

"Give it a week," she says. "Maybe longer, if he broke something. Enough to get you back on your feet, ready to handle things. That happens, we head back over there. Remind Nag' of his obligations."

Wanton coughs, spits blood into the gutter. "Can't say I won't look forward to that."

They walk another block before she asks: "Do you remember it?"

Wanton lifts his head. Remember what?"

"The sleep," she says. "The passage of years. For real, this time, don't fuck with me."

He can't walk, while he thinks on it. Just becomes a dead weight on her shoulder. She lowers him to the ground, up against a low wall. Sits down beside him and takes a breather.

"You know," Wanton says, "I don't really remember shit. I just remember coming out, the bright lights and the sure-as-shit confusion. The shit that went down after, once they explained how things would be."

"Yeah," Cody says. "Yeah. That sounds familiar."

Wanton shifts his leg, winces a little. "We really going to lean on Nag?"

She nods. "Man owes us for making him king," she says. "An' someone out there can do what we can't. Figure we should talk to him, now we know what he charges. Ain't going to do us any good, but, well, you know…"

For a moment Wanton just wheezes through the bloody wreck of his nose. Then it clicks into place, and the big man is smiling through the carnage that used to be his face. She stands, gets him up again. Helps him get moving.

Wanton keeps smiling the whole damn way home.

# ABOUT THE AUTHOR

PETER M. BALL is an author, publisher, and RPG gamer whose love of speculative fiction emerged after exposure to *The Hobbit*, *Star Wars*, David Lynch's *Dune*, and far too many games of *Dungeons and Dragons* before the age of 7. He's spent the bulk of his life working as a creative writing tutor, with brief stints as a performance poet, gaming convention organiser, online content developer, non-profit arts manager, GenreCon convenor, and d20 RPG publisher.

He's the author of the Miriam Aster series and the Keith Murphy Urban Fantasy Thrillers, three short story collections, and more stories, articles, poems, and RPG material than he'd care to count.

He's the brain-in-charge at Brain Jar Press, an aspiring made scientist running publishing experiments through Eclectic Projects, and resides in Brisbane, Australia, with his partner and a very affectionate cat.

Find Peter Online at PeterMBall.com *or reach out to Peter on your favourite Social Media platforms:*

facebook.com/PeterMBall

twitter.com/PeterMBall

instagram.com/PeterMBall

goodreads.com/PeterMBall

patreon.com/PeterMBall

# LOOKING FOR ANOTHER GREAT SCIENCE FICTION READ?

The twelve stories in Not Quite The End Of The World Just Yet showcase Peter M. Ball at his best. The tales touch upon science fiction, horror, and fantasy, but all see people brush against the sublime and discover who they truly are.

The collection includes the Aurealis Award winning "Clockwork, Patchwork, and Raven," the very first tale set in Helix City. Here, a clockwork man dreams of a fairy-tale ending while trying to protect those he loves from a dangerous gang of genetically engineered crow boys.

---

If you'd like a taste of where it all started, turn the page for an preview from *Not Quite The End Of The World Just Yet...*

# CLOCKWORK, PATCHWORK, & RAVEN

## A SHORT STORY EXCERPT FROM NOT QUITE THE END OF THE WORLD JUST YET

Jackson said she'd been hanging with the Corvidae before he found her, that she was one of those girls that bounced between gangers named Jackdaw6 or Raven8. They'd pumped her full of genemorphs laced with avian DNA, hoping she'd be lucky and avoid the bad reaction. It had already affected her teeth, turning the molars into rotting shards. Her lips were growing hard, thickening into dark cartilage, and I could see the shadow of her organs beneath the bleached skin stretched across her ribcage. Jackson said he found her wandering in the alley behind the crow boy's nest, trying to staunch the fluid seeping from her fresh-plucked eye-socket. He brought her home, patched her up, and turned her over to me for safe-keeping while he went downstairs to work. I stood over her and watched her, letting the hours tick by, and eventually I kissed her.

My kiss didn't wake her, though she stirred a little at my touch. Downside is not a place where fairytales happen, and no-one would mistake me for a handsome prince. It was a clumsy kiss, as you'd expect, but a kiss. A kiss!

When she did not wake I stood, resuming my vigil. I could

feel myself blushing, my right cheek warm. I turned my other cheek towards her, hiding behind the copper mask.

Even now, looking back, I'm still not sure why I did it. It's not as if she was a pretty thing, with her bruises and her missing eye, but there was still some remnant of beauty beneath the blue stitches of Jackson's repair. She was a creature of the Downside streets, all feral promise and rough allure. I didn't love her – that would be unseemly for a half-man like me – but I envied her, desperately, for the blue stitching that held her together and the heart that still beat in her chest. I wished, for just a moment, that Jackson had done the same for me. I could feel the steady flick of that pulse when our lips touched. It was alive; faint, but eager to exist. My own heart ticked on, steady and regular, the soft tick-tock marking a regular beat as it pulped blood through those veins I still possessed.

Jackson wanted to be a hero, I knew that without asking. When I was little, just after he took me in, Jackson used to tell me stories about heroes, about knights and princes and ducks that turned into swans. I would listen to his stories, curled up in bed, crying as the pain of a new graft wracked my chest and shoulder. I had to ignore the sound of the gangs and the crowds that filled the Downside streets, the occasional brawl or gunshot cutting through the din. Jackson would fill my head with heroes, with worlds where heroes still existed. I never believed in his stories, but I always believed in Jackson. It was easier, cleaner, but it was just as dangerous in the end…

———

This story and eleven more can be found in *Not Quite The End Of the World Just Yet*, Peter M. Ball's second collection from Brain Jar Press. Available direct from the publisher and from all good bookstores.

# ALSO BY PETER M. BALL

### SHORT STORY COLLECTIONS

The Birdcage Heart & Other Strange Tales

Not Quite The End Of the World Just Yet: Short Stories & Strange Futures

These Strange & Magic Things: Short Stories

### MIRIAM ASTER NOVELLAS

Horn

Bleed

### BRAIN JAR PRESS SHORT FICTION LAB

The Early Experiments

Winged, With Sharp Teeth

8 Minutes Of Usable Daylight

A White Cross Beside A Lonely Road

One Last First Date Before The End Of The World

Shedding Skins

### ESSAYS

You Don't Want To Be Published & Other Things Nobody Tells You When You First Start Writing

# THANK YOU FOR BUYING THIS ECLECTIC PROJECTS CHAPBOOK

To receive special offers, bonus content, and info on new releases and other great reads, sign up for our newsletters.

To get more from the author, Peter M. Ball, you can sign up for his newsletter at PeterMBall.com